CW01652453

ATLANTIC

KELLEY SWAIN

Cinnamon Press
INDEPENDENT INNOVATIVE INTERNATIONAL

Published by Cinnamon Press
Meirion House,
Glan yr afon,
Tanygrisiau,
Blaenau Ffestiniog,
Gwynedd, LL41 3SU
www.cinnamonpress.com

The right of Kelley Swain to be identified as author of this work has been asserted by her in accordance with the Copyright, Designs and Patent Act, 1988. Copyright © 2014 Kelley Swain
ISBN: 978-1-909077-23-2

British Library Cataloguing in Publication Data. A CIP record for this book can be obtained from the British Library.

All rights reserved. No part of this publication may be reproduced, stored in a retrieval system, or transmitted in any form or by any means, electronic, mechanical, photocopying, recording or otherwise without the prior written permission of the publishers. This book may not be lent, hired out, resold or otherwise disposed of by way of trade in any form of binding or cover other than that in which it is published, without the prior consent of the publishers.

Designed and typeset in Palatino by Cinnamon Press
Cover from original artwork 'Structuur' by Henrike Scholten © Henrike Scholten. Used with kind permission
Cover design by Jan Fortune

Printed in Poland

Cinnamon Press is represented in the UK by Inpress Ltd www.inpressbooks.co.uk and in Wales by the Welsh Books Council www.cllc.org.uk

Acknowledgments

Special thanks to the Nevada Street Poets (Mick Delap, Malene Engelund, Lorraine Mariner, Dominic McLoughlin, David Nash, and Sarah Westcott,) for critiques, wine, and friendship, to Richard Barnett for edits and inspiration, and to Henrike Scholten for her cover art. Warm thanks to Jan Fortune for her guidance and enthusiasm in publishing this book.

Acknowledgement is due to *The Rialto* for first publishing 'Work the Bass, Lay me Down'; to *The Human Genre Project* for 'Jargon'; to *The London Magazine* for 'The Shop of Reclaimed Windows'; to *Bliss* Templar poetry anthology for 'Utility with an *F*'; to *Lung Jazz: Young British Poets for Oxfam* for 'Questions of Travel'; to *The Junket* and Badaude for 'Sestina: Frimaire'.

Contents

'And from the plank, far shatter'd o'er the rocks,
Build me a little bark of hope, once more
To battle with the ocean and the shocks
Of the loud breakers, and the ceaseless roar
Which rushes on the solitary shore'

Byron

In Memoriam

Nancy Perry Kelley
1924 – 2011
&
Harmon 'Rockie' Kelley
1920 – 2011

Atlantic

Archaeologist

Sift the sand,
the grains of her life.

You will find bones.

Shake the sieve
that holds her –

          there, a shred
of luck,

and when the sun hits
just right,
          the glint
of golden times.

Handle those fragments
with care.

          Here, the crockery
of broken hearts.

No matter
how you tilt it,

through even
the finest weave
slips a shade:

What she always felt
          was missing.

The Maiden

The one with violets in her lap weeps for joy of sun,
triumph through clouds on the first of March.

The flowers beneath her hands, dead, wilted dry,
crumble from wind, mournful winter dark.

But it is come, brushing fingers of light,
gilding hair and eyelids, and she dusts

crushed petals from her skirt, stands,
steps outdoors into spring's embrace.

'Chestita Baba Marta' they say, winding wool
of red and white round wrists and fine tree limbs

welcoming rebirth, feeling the ancient certainty
of its return. All will bloom; hair will spin to gold,

cloaks and shawls will drop away, warmth will reach
lips and buds. Violets will grow again. She will draw

them close, plucking gently, tracing each stem
from ripening earth, gathering the bouquet.

Work the Bass, Lay me Down

Yes, I'm imagining you naked
as the sax swoons,
splays across my ear.

Oh yes, I'm thinking of your
long thighs, flat stomach,
as the brass shivers.

The notes dance your silhouette,
lean and silken,
and my guts strain towards you.

Trumpet sighs,
we lie; pale pair of drumsticks.
rat-a-tat-tat.

The sultry wink
of copper catches the light;
your blue eyes.

My flesh ripples
at the touch of cool notes,
your staccato angles.

Ah-one, Ah-two, Ah-one two three.
The long slide
of the trombone.

Then, silence.
I almost want
a cigarette.

Lavare

They were fighting today.
For 'they' I wanted to say 'Seraphs'.

But they were wood pigeons. Two feathers
of tiniest hook-and-eye down, on the candle
in the window, above the washroom sink.

Simple. Two feathers.
Simple?

My absence, until then,
my inability to observe
their arrival, overwhelms
the water running from the tap;
gutters the flame.

They left remnants of wings.
They moulted in their sleep.

Tube

Fleshed and compressed
on the Underground.

Don't say 'like sardines'
we're not aquatic;

beyond tectonic,
gnawing through rock,

rattling Roman bones
as we rattle our own.

Young Leda

She's twelve; strapped down
to a knee-board behind a boat, riding
the wake of its roaring engine,
motoring across Wyassup Lake.

She thinks it clever to aim for a flock
of Canada Geese. Rope taut,
coasting near, tilting her body
into that feathered assembly,

they take off, scattering – all but one,
too slow – it catches in the net
of her lap, flapping, and she won't cry
out, but closes her eyes, holds on, flies

across the water, wings beating her face,
a panic of limbs, until she yields, leans back –
and it flies away, leaving empty space,
her eyes, her self, intact.

Jargon

My father's angina, we learned, was a serious myocardial infarction
caused by coronary thrombosis, possibly due to atherosclerosis
but more likely unlucky genetic inheritance, potentially preceded
by acute depression brought on by Seasonal Affective Disorder,
migration north from the Caribbean to cold New England,
Vitamin D deficiency, low melatonin levels,
low serotonin neurotransmitters;
low self-esteem, all leading to
ventricular fibrillation,
heart attack,
death.

Renovation

later, Mom
obliterated the wall
where he fell.

The Shop of Reclaimed Windows

Junk shop handles
like so many doors to nowhere—
tinned faces, and a fan spreading
irises of air.

Prisms hallucinating
beside a soft smell of wood, rust,
parallels and mirrors;
'Dreams' nailed to a wall.

His was a palace like this,
and the old barn holds his smell:
the grease, the sawdust,
the cool isolation.

I am Alice, lost
in the kaleidoscope—
windows, doors, bathtub drains,
rusted gates and sunset panes.

I lurch up dusty stairs
expecting to see my father—
but there are only doors, doors
and windows, all leading, all looking,
to walls.

Bearings

Dad's soul may not be 'up there' somewhere, peering down,
but he looked into the night sky: he knew these constellations.

Orion, Big Dipper, Andromeda, Pegasus.
He sailed north by them with mom.

When the electrics failed on the *Saracen,* Captain Jack
guided her safely from St. Thomas to Rhode Island.

*

We planned to throw Dad's ashes into the bay at St. Thomas,
but now they rest in the prettiest bit of real estate in Rhode Island,

overlooking the Pawcatuck River,
heading out to sea, to Napatree Point,

*

where we pushed into the sandbar with our toes,
clam-digging for chowder,

where I pulled up an enormous spider crab,
screamed, and heaved it into the waves.

Dad laughed. He looked up at the moon,
like I do now. The moon that pulls

those tides and waves,
builds the sandbar, destroys, builds it again.

Monument

To us,
stone endures.

Comes from earth,
is earth.

Wears, like us,
but more slowly,

words weathering
to whispers,

fading faces
of granite.

Yet lasting
enough

so we feel
we leave

a certainty
behind.

Sketch

The man in the life drawing class who cannot breathe
on anything but roll-ups, who leaves every twenty minutes
with crumpled green bags of tobacco, but somehow
does not smell of smoke: he inhales, exhales, with a whirr,
the thrum of a consumptive yogi; strangely comforting.

I sit nude on a wooden desk draped with pastel-smudged cloth.
My breasts ache, moon-heavy, wanting to sprout ivy vines,
or milk; but I stop their bloom with a cornucopia of pills
to smother fruit whose weight I will not bear.

To the class I am only a figure, to sketch.

The Indian woman stands in a beam of window-light,
and though my head is angled so I cannot see her,
my eye glimpses her shadow across the wood floor's gloss:
one arm, twelve panes of light, a square of paper,
moving, shifting; her arm-shadow drawing a negative of me.

My back aches as I sit, but not as my grandmother aches,
her bones grating against each other, the muscles in her neck
clutching until she screams. I hear her cries echoing
across the Atlantic.

At the break, they leave for coffee;
the man goes for a smoke, leaving a pile of eraser crumbs,
pencil shavings, tobacco dust. In my robe, I pace the room,
look at the figures sketched onto sugar-paper. My head
is an afterthought, a vague egg. Figure drawing: not portrait.

But the man who cannot breathe has sketched only my face,
looking down, away to the left, and it is me.
The explosion of eraser crumbs, to be blown or brushed away,
lie on the paper, a static cloud bursting from my forehead,
wheeling like a flock of birds seen high in the air.

Is the smoking man killing himself quickly,
or preserving himself slowly? What happens
to these pictures he draws?

The class returns. I sit.

My grandmother's cartilage has abandoned her.
I have abandoned her. If these thoughts could wheel
from my head, a flock of birds; eraser crumbs.
If my grandmother could have been fixed on sugar-paper
at twenty-five, only aching with fertility and impatience.

The thrum of the man's breath; the flicker of window-light.
He leaves early, abandoning his pile of pencil shavings,
eraser crumbs, tobacco dust.

Mimicry

You flit
on the surfaces

— a manic
butterfly—

rapt
in weak oscillations

trapped

by opaque fenestrations

– unable
to move
beyond

your version

of a smile.

Firebird

I want to smother this phoenix
before it bursts into its riot of flame:
wrap my hands around its golden beak,
smooth my thumbs underneath,
singeing my fingertips, pressing
into that velvet throat
ringed with sapphire and red opal –
throttle the goddamn bird
with all its false, recurring hope,
all its persistence
its denial of mortality –
snuff the life out
before it can spark, insistent,
lighting my eyes again.

Utility with an 'F'

is me on my knees holding a torch with my head stuck in the
washing machine
trying to see if that fucking plastic tab from your collared shirt is the
culprit
of that horrid rasping sound,
and if we do need to buy a new one, whether it should be
a Bosch like this one or a Zanussi or that really cheap one
that still got good reviews,

and remember *Etera*, the village in Bulgaria,
where everything from the wood-carver's wheel to the jeweller's
blow-torch
drew its power from fast-flowing mountain water,
where people from near and far brought their rugs, in richest ochre,
indigo, red,
to the wooden outdoor tub, pounding with icy water—
no detergent, no Woolite or Limelite
—just cold fresh water—
never shrinking the wool, never draining the colours.

Urban Fox

Sleep, little russet one,
with your fleas,
your broken tail, your sharp
smile, as Southeastern
creaks and squeals
past your sunny leaf-bank;
dream of rubbish bins
tipped by wind, spilling
Thursday-night tikkas
and Friday-night pizzas;
dream of green fields
and silent wide spaces
till dawn.

Questions of Travel

after Bishop

Let me shed these smothering albatrosses
as I cross the Atlantic.

Let me moult these heavinesses
from my neck as I wing west.

The greatest furies can astonish, bring peace
in the smallest gesture, as palm to palm

is holy palmers' kiss. Give me your hand, then,
and bring me calm as you bring me storms

which sweep me from my founderings.
I'm learning all the ways to drown.

The Waves

soporific; somnambulistic
sleep, sleep.

you crash on me

(but I have so missed the sea,
its power is unexpected.)

we walk together, touching
(sleep, sleep.)

I wake alone, wet
brackish with tides.

Cartography

Gran in hospital, eighty-six.
Gramps, eighty-nine, at home – afraid.

That he could fear anything, this explorer
who travelled from Siberia to Auschwitz
to other hearts of darkness,
'the first white man some natives ever saw'.

My aunts and uncles, the five Medician Stars,
ellipse them like planetary moons.

I'm the young one in this orrery,
still far enough from the horizon
to think the Earth is flat.
To know time goes on forever.

Haversham Pond

For Nancy Perry Kelley, Christmas 2010

She creaks in ossified lace,
porous, marvelling. *Europa*
hides an ocean, Gran – she
will refuse to believe it.

And how could I dream
of that satellite when tethered
to this orbit: skin of bark,
leathered books. Home.

She told me this golden
November morning, last night
she dreamt of swimming:
Haversham Pond. My mother

passed in a boat, threw a rope:

Gran lifted, a swan.

Anchor

For Harmon 'Rockie' Kelley, and Four Margin Street, May 2011

This house is a ship coming into the break-yard.
She's stayed her course since 1848.
While four generations planed, caulked and kept,
he built the hearth of the home standing now.

Three generations help lay him down.
No Pierce-Arrow Limos, no more red canoe.
While three sailing boats sink into yuccas,
no cords of wood insulate us from snow.

These leagues of darkness unbalance the compass.
The riptide may take us, from just off the shore.
What family remains, waits: swallows salt.

He always planned to go down with his ship.
They sink together, while one purple beech tree
bows near the deck. And all are at rest,
save us, treading water.

Posy

Water rules; they bow to it. A pigment, a fingerprint, a fragment.
We are all become this: a drop of water.

The fallen petals in my pocket suffer under the gentlest handling.
Droplets tick through the flora.

I sit, not waiting for the rain to cease, or for night to fall.
Only to sit, beneath an umbrella, surrounded by roses.

I lay my grief there. The plants will carry on, tended by a host
of insects, rifled by pigeons, robins, crows, subject only to August.

The bees and bee-flies will have their sugar; the air and earth,
their perfume. My eyes collect their colour, but cannot hold it,

cannot carry their pigment as far as a glance away.
White, yellow, orange, pink, red: not a fact, but an idea,

a spectrum of all the whites there could be, from crisp linen
to tawny limestone; all the yellows: canary, sun-rich, saffron or pale;

a gingham dress in summertime on the one you love, or on you.
All oranges: fire, fruit, sunburn, leather.

All pinks: raw steak, kissed lips, my grandmother's handbag.
Rain eases. Birds begin conversations. Insects attend my notebook.

I plant my grief in the rose garden.
What petals, what petals are these?

Snow White's Fever

It took her three days to dissolve.

Her stomach relinquished all claims
to appetite: water has no mouth.

Bitter ache, chill ache. No ache
could spark her tongue.

The meat of words sank into her mattress.

She was spangled; particulate.
But who could revive her? Too many
helpers, and the Prince didn't know his chemistry.

If she could only feel warm (all the while
she was burning) enough to evaporate –

could some salt of her
be scraped together, returned to her lips?

Wings

This house heard recently the beating of wings.
Witnessed, only hours ago, a disturbance. Evidence
across the bedroom tiles: rain of blood, droppings.
Then nothing. Two black cats sleeping on the bed.
The ticking heartbeat of all the unmatched
clocks in the house spoke of tangled air;
all the doors and windows shut. Whether this
unlucky paraclete had been brought, or sent,
I found it lying on the carpet in the sun,
red-breasted, punctured. Not a gift I wanted.
And surely only trouble comes from winged,
uninvited guests, leaving bloody traces.

Inheritance

Freud is everywhere. But with a bob, and petite:
like my grandmother.

Once, when her best friend married a man she couldn't stand,
she stopped speaking to her friend until the day that husband died.

The fury came, Mom tells me, when people didn't follow the plans
she'd quietly constructed in her mind.

Should I wish to be more like my grandfather, calmly gutting fish
on the dock, away from the house, but within ear's reach?

He was the one who killed men, in the war, in Germany.
But he never spoke of it, and I never dared ask.

The Dream

My friend who has lately died of cancer and I
fly above a blackened and turbulent ocean
and there is some necessity of leaping from the belly of the plane
there is screaming wind; lashing whitecaps beneath
someone is urging *jump, jump*
I feel a primal fear, hear the words of my father (also dead)
I see no point in jumping from a perfectly good airplane

and I cannot let go
but my friend is already gone.

Ten-Year Anniversary

When we come upon the season
of mellow mists and misty moors,
all the clichés that absolve us of our sorrows,
I do think more often of the dead.

When the world dies beautifully around me,
forgive me for thinking you have turned
into an oak, copper beech, or chestnut:
it is the compromise for letting you go.

The greatest violence I've known
was seeing you in your coffin.

Conduct me to the woods
where I can think you into being.

Pigeon on Glass

What's it like to be unafraid
Of approaching a steep edge?
Trusting one can stretch
And be buoyed by air?
Not even the hesitancy of Icarus
When he first lifted off,
But an inherent assurance
That no matter how hard the ground,
One won't be bruised or broken.

Sestina: Frimaire

There's a cloven-hooved print dried into the mud,
and it's not Pan. They've gone topsy-turvy, wrecked
the garden. What if they insisted on staying?
Would it be any better than fly-by-night destruction?
Rinsing brain-ridges on a *choufleur* form
has been called meditative. But the state

of things! Macerated. Is it a statement
if no one listens? One thousand muddy
pairs of boots settle, take up pitchforks, form
a queue. Back at the kitchen basin: wreck
of *genièvre,* honeyed flowers, a destruction
of macerated plants. *Will you be staying?*

Camomile calm, to think of staying
here. 'To Be.' A woe-rilled, wax-malleable state
held at arm's-length with canapés. Destruction:
foie gras, olives farcies, michette, moules. Pâté de boue.
Open the shutters. This wrecking
light which cuts out each cedar and pine form

strips everything bare. True to form,
nothing but the trees will be staying
the same. But can gorse balm ease the wreck
of lost faith? And if 'faith' was never the state
of one's disposition? If only earth and mud
are real. Each *santon* a hand-crafted destruction

pricking tiny barbs from each window. Destruction
of tidy, terraced trees and flower-beds forming
hillside gardens, *sangliers* reduced to porcelain crèche; mud-
painted hoof-prints of roe deer, wild boar; tableaux staying
the same year after year. What is there to heal? State
of mind? State of heart? Wrecked faith or wrecked

hope? Or everything precious to hand; naught wrecked
at all. Picasso's *Hibou,* Van Gogh's *Cypresses;* destruction
at bay in azure, purple, blue. *Herbes* deconstructed:
garlic, sage, for the feast; lavender for the crucifix form;
olives, milk, honey in the shower: scents staying
on skin, in hair, day to day. Bath salts and mud

masks; salt of the earth. Stately herbs, racked
and dried. Mud-rich earth, destroyed,
re-built, re-formed. This earth claims us, makes us stay.

Oxford Parks

15 Feb, after visiting Hepworth sculptures in the Ashmolean

Is this what they mean by 'water meadow'?

Drowning willows

Birds claiming | declaiming.

Fertilist mud,

Nine degrees in air | all change:

Green   Yellow   Waking

Squabbling   Spring

Castle 8

After Simone Weil and Geoffrey Hill

I love your satisfaction
and I love your desire

desire most fulfilling
nothing cold in fire

you fulfil my sorrow
for my heart is prey

my sparrowhawk
your sparrow

everything you say

Apologia

You bring violence and myrrh,
gifts of passion that lack
a middle name. We have
travelled far. Coming home
to this, our new, old island,
land of rain, of mist.

This rage of love born
from unhappy time. Solitude,
our catalyst. Why we need
an arm's-length, even when
tangled as one. Why each
overripe persimmon carries
no surprise. How the holy
incense intoxicates, then burns.

My exile has proven this:
My body needs your love to live.
My hand, freedom, to write.

Sweetening the Garlic

You say you're only deft below the wrist. You pluck each clove,
undress the paper shells, peel until you reach flesh,
but that's only the beginning. You open it to the bud;
take out the green centre. *To remove the bitterness.*
Bringing tears to my eyes.

What shall we call it? Not a diminishing; an adding.
Not un-bittering, but sweetening the garlic.
Can I taste my carelessness in the kitchen
against your quiet precision? I know this:
our feasts are the sweetest I've had.

Unbuckling the Hunter's Belt

Focus on distant Orion, my fingers rest upon, flicker.

Day is night, crows, wood-pigeons, sing us: bed down,
your fingers in my hair, mouth: sweet riches,

a drunken autumn; an exquisite solstice. Where
are the deepest reaches? Elude discovery:

lead me to your delicious dark soapy-full
salt-warmth and blazing, blazing constellations.

In the British Museum

I met a traveller from an antique land
Who said: Two vast and trunkless legs of stone
Stand in the desart.

You read 'Ozymandias' into my ear, breath of iambs
For me and me alone.

And there we stand, gazing on the desert-roughened
Granite that sanded Shelley's mind.
Your arms wrap from behind, your lip upon my ear.

If Ramesses was a Trojan horse I'd drag you inside and –
But instead we stroll through halls of clocks,

Your hand commanding treasures (silk suspenders)
Stretching sands (a cashmere dress)
Boundless passions (my lace-bound breasts).

Look on my works, ye Mighty, and despair.

Artichoke

Eating the oily, chargrilled thistle
I remember riding you amidst the trees,

the horses, the hallooing pheasants
of Windsor Great Park.

Bellowing stags: the autumn rut,
sticks against my knees, your back.

Our picnic, deep in the woods.
Ourselves, deep in each other.

Now, late winter,
we gorge on these hearts together.

Babel

I don't want you with me each moment.
We can't even bear ourselves, always.

But I want you with me now. And if I wrote,
'I want you with me now,' each time I thought it,
I could fill the shelves of the Library of Babel: endless volumes.

Endless volumes, shelves and shelves insensible.
Which we fill volumes to try, to fail, to explain. Lover,
we have our own language: our fingers, our tongues, our bodies.
Working the page, working the sheets, working each other.

Your ink brands me and I swallow your sentences whole.

Helen of Troy in the Bath

There's an old claw-foot, blue, with brass taps.
The handles fall off when I turn.
But enough hot water to shame a mortal in this age of austerity.

I add bubbles.
I like my wine almost black, tasting of ashes,
a cremation of grapes.

Disrobing, I slide in. Flush pink, hands and feet screaming.
Why the British keep their homes so cold, I'll never understand.
Your climate fosters a morbid disposition.
Melancholia. Poetry.

'Fathomed'. It's a good word.
Though when it comes down to the act,
a woman wants to be made love to, or fucked.

I run my hands over my breasts, fathoming.
It's the sort of tub for fathoms.

Conjuring forty toy ships, I let them float.
They'll founder near the islands of my thighs.
Perhaps every man yearns to be Odysseus.
Then despite it all, his marriage wouldn't run aground.

The tap chokes. What is it we wish to comprehend?
Love? Everyone always writes and rewrites
the story of my mother. We can see there's enough lust
to go around, but not where one needs it.

For heaven's sake, my ancestors were screwing geese.
Swans.

Tell Mephistopheles I'll magick my own illusions:
like these ships, listing in my coils of hair –
and all those tiny souls on board.

I take up a razor, warm it in the hot water.
Sometimes it's pinfeathers the blade scrapes
from my legs and underarms. Don't tell.
I'd say they're white as snow, but I could be lying.

The wine, the bubbles, make me giddy:
I'll pull the plug, watch my forty ships
spiral, and spiral,
          and spiral down the drain.

Atlantic

She divides her time between one side
and another, counting, the beads of her abacus
wampum, winkles, and sandpiper skulls.
She has the power to add, to take away;
        she breathes with the moon.

Deaf to the wails of the lost,
of those who seek sirens,
or flee them, she sometimes mates
with the wind, to bear a storm;
        to drown out the cries.

Her loss is greater than their weight
in bones, for she can never be whole.
Fleeting rides with the ferrymen
remind her of time. Of counting.
        Wampum, winkles, and sand.

She sings her dirge to the skulls
of birds, plaiting the rushes and sea-weeds.
Only the abacus knows her sorrow
as she weeps, fingering each orbit
        on her hollow rosary.

Kelley Swain was born during a blizzard in Westerly, Rhode Island, in 1985. In 2007 she graduated from Randolph-Macon Woman's College in Virginia with a BA in English and a minor in Environmental Studies. In her final year she was also able to study biology, evolution, animal behaviour, zoology, and geology. She went on to complete the Munson Institute for Maritime Studies summer graduate programme at the Mystic Seaport (CT) and focused on the history of cetology in Moby-Dick. Kelley moved to London in late summer 2007. She was Poet-in-Residence at the Whipple Museum of the History of Science, Department of the History and Philosophy of Science, Cambridge, from 2009 - 2012, and is a Fellow of the Linnean Society of London. She is currently a guest lecturer in Medical Humanities for Imperial College London's Global Health BSc. Her debut collection, *Darwin's Microscope,* was published by Flambard Press in 2009. She is editor of the anthology *Pocket Horizon,* published by Valley Press in 2013. Her verse drama, *Opera di Cera,* about the anatomical wax models of La Specola, Florence, was published by Valley Press in 2014. Her pamphlet, *Women, Astronomy, and Greenwich,* was published by the Royal Society & Royal Observatory Greenwich in 2010, and her historical novel, *Double the Stars,* based on the life of the astronomer Caroline Herschel, was shortlisted in the Cinnamon Press Novel Awards and will be published by Cinnamon in autumn 2014. Kelley is currently working on *The Naked Muse,* a memoir of her experiences as an artists' model.

Henrike Scholten is a visual artist from the Netherlands. She lives and works in Groningen, whilst studying and exhibiting internationally.

She mainly works with coloured pencils, creating intricate drawings on paper. Her drawings present an ambiguous sense of scale and materiality, shapes suspended between movement and stillness, corporeality and immateriality.

The picture on the cover of this book is entitled *Structuur*, the first of an on-going series of large drawings. It was made in 2011 and measures 100 x 150 cm. The drawing *Structuur* was influenced by Henrike's studies of medical museum specimens, as well as Hokusai's famous print, *The Great Wave off Kanagawa*.

Structuur and other drawings can be found online at www.henrikescholten.nl